Anonymous

Lilia

A drama

Anonymous

Lilia
A drama

ISBN/EAN: 9783337383510

Printed in Europe, USA, Canada, Australia, Japan

Cover: Foto ©Andreas Hilbeck / pixelio.de

More available books at **www.hansebooks.com**

LILIA;

OR,

The Test.

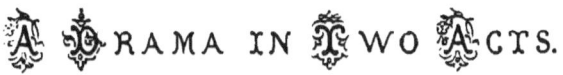

A DRAMA IN TWO ACTS.

Translated from the French

BY LILLY FOLEY.

And Respectfully Dedicated

To the Catholic Academies of Chicago.

BALTIMORE:

Published by John Murphy & Co.

New-York. Catholic Publication Society.

MDCCCLXX.

CHARACTERS.

Madame DE ST. ELME, a rich widow.

LILIA, her adopted daughter.

MARGARET, Lilia's mother.

VIRGINIA,
DELPHINA, } young girls of the village.

LISETTA,
MARIETTA, } little villagers.

Miss JOSEPHINE, a friend of Madame de St. Elme.

Mrs. ROGER, the housekeeper.

ANNETTE, a waiting-maid.

The scene is laid at the entrance of Madame de St. Elme's castle.

LILIA.

ACT I.

SCENE I.—*Madame de St. Elme—Miss Josephine.*

MISS JOSEPHINE. Ah! my dear friend, always sad and thoughtful! I hoped that the pure air of the country and the beauties of nature would drive away the dismal melancholy to which you have for some time been a prey.

MADAME DE ST. ELME. No, my dear Josephine, the beauty of nature can do nothing for me. The disease which is consuming me, is too deeply rooted; it is incurable.

MISS JOSEPHINE. You distress me. What, then, is this malady which is consuming you? Is your health seriously affected? I fear so, because you are visibly failing.

MADAME DE ST. ELME. Be assured, my dear friend, my health is good enough, but my poor heart is very sick. That child whom I have adopted, to whom I have promised a mother's love . . . . .

MISS JOSEPHINE. Well!

MADAME DE ST. ELME. She is no longer the same. The sweet virtues which rendered her so amiable to my eyes, have given place to vanity, pride, and frivolity.

MISS JOSEPHINE When did you perceive this fatal change?

MADAME DE ST. ELME. After her return from the castle of Cérigny. The marchioness urged me with so many entreaties to intrust her to her, to pass the coming vacation with her young daughter, who had been her intimate friend at school; she herself appeared to desire it with so much ardor, that I consented, rejoicing to have procured some weeks of pleasure for her. O fatal journey! It has destroyed my happiness!

MISS JOSEPHINE. It is possible that she may have imbibed in that family ideas contrary to the solid principles in which you have reared her; but you think the evil to be greater than it is.

MADAME DE ST. ELME. No, my friend. Unhappily, I do not deceive myself. She was formerly pious, modest, studious, meek, and compassionate to the miseries of the poor; now she is proud and scornful to the good villagers who surround her with their attentions, exacting and cruel to the servants, fickle and careless. In a word, she used to be loved everywhere, and now her conduct can only alienate all hearts from her.

MISS JOSEPHINE. Has she changed in respect to you?

MADAME DE ST. ELME. Not absolutely. She believes me to be her mother, and I am still the principal object of her affections; however, I no longer suffice for her. In her childhood, and afterwards when she had left school, she was never happy except when near me. She worked gaily by my side, and a walk taken together was the most agreeable recreation I could procure for her. How many times, then, after having passed part of the day with her young companions, did she cast herself into my arms, saying: "Ah! mamma, far from you I cannot be happy. How long the day has seemed to me, in the midst of my games and other pleasures!" It is not thus now; domestic happiness no longer exists for her. She must dress, have company, and attend soirées. She dreams only of all these frivolities, and already I have seen her cry and pout, because I have refused to take her to the theatre.

MISS JOSEPHINE. This change is unfortunate; however, ...

MADAME DE ST. ELME. Wait, my friend, I must tell you all. God has, without doubt, given me no children so that my immense fortune may be the patrimony of the unfortunate, and, at the death of my husband, I thought of retiring from the world and formed many projects of charitable establishments. Instead of following these good inspirations, I concentrated all my affections on one only object, and wished to experience the feelings of a mother. I

1*

adopted this child, and I have loved her with a mother's love. For a long time she corresponded to my tenderness, and I have tasted an unspeakable happiness. With joy, I saw her merit my benefits, and I formed sweet projects for the future. I would grow old surrounded by her care and affection, I said to myself, and after my death she will continue the good that I do. . . . . But to-day, the saddest reflections have assailed me. This young girl can make me happy no longer. Heaven is punishing me! I took her away from her mother when she was her treasure—she will be my sorrow. . . . Poor mother! Misery had forced her husband to enlist in the army in the place of the son of a rich proprietor of the country, and he was on the point of starting. Touched by the despair of this unhappy woman and enchanted by the beauty of her little daughter, I proposed to ransom her husband, if she would consent to resign her daughter to me. After several combats in her mind between conjugal and maternal love, she gave me this poor little girl and swore never to make herself known. I gave the young couple a sum of money, which they put with some other cash; then I left the country, and never heard of them any more. On arriving this year, I learned, with pain, that the man was dead. His poor widow, alone and forsaken, regrets, without doubt, the arrangement which she has made, because she is a stranger and has no relations in this country. Ah! it would have been more generous to have helped her without depriving her of her child. I would now enjoy their gratitude; they would bless me whilst loving each other, and the young girl might have been preserved, by labor and poverty, from the vices which are now taking possession of her heart. . . . . I cannot express to you how hard the trial is when I meet this poor woman and see her look at her child, whilst heaving deep sighs. It seems to me that her look is one of cruel reproach which pierces my soul.

MISS JOSEPHINE. Why should she reproach you? You have fulfilled your engagement with her. Has she sought to speak to you?

MADAME DE ST. ELME. Twice she has advanced towards me, and I believed that she was going to speak; but I suppose she was afraid to do so.

MISS JOSEPHINE. I believe, my dear Ambroisine, that the sight of this poor woman is painful to you, and I am astonished that you came here, knowing that you would certainly see her. You had reason to fear that she would make herself known to her child and bring new troubles upon you.

MADAME DE ST. ELME. Irritated by the change which has taken place in Lilia, and reproaching myself for my foolish tenderness and extravagance towards her, I had resolved to restore her to her mother, insuring to her an honest support, because I have not reared her to bear hard labor, and I would reproach myself for having made her unhappy. I hoped to be able, then, to break off all communication with them, and, at length, to find again a little peace. But since my arrival, my heart is so troubled that I feel incapable of keeping my resolution.

Miss Josephine.   I believe, my friend.....

SCENE II.—*The same—Annette.*

Annette, (*entering.*) Elizabeth desires to speak to you, madame.

Madame de St. Elme. I will go to her. Come, my dear Josephine. It may be necessary for me to go to the farm, and, as we walk together, I will consult with you upon a plan I have formed. (*They retire.*)

SCENE III.—*Annette, alone.*

Annette.   I do not know what makes Madame de St. Elme so sad of late. No one would know her now..... And Miss Lilia, formerly so bright, so gay, so good, has become inaccessible, nothing gives her pleasure, she is all the time in a bad humor..... It must be that they have met with some misfortune. Perhaps they have lost all their money...... Too many persons are ruined now-a-days, to wonder at anything..... Whatever it may be, if this continue, the house will no longer be endurable. I shall be obliged to leave it..... But here comes Miss Lilia.

SCENE IV.—*Annette—Lilia.*

LILIA, (*entering.*) I thought mamma was here.

ANNETTE. She has gone out, miss.

LILIA. Miss Josephine is with her, without doubt.

ANNETTE. Yes, miss, they have gone to the farm.

LILIA. I did not ask you where they had gone. What a habit this is you have taken of questioning every body and of meddling with every thing!

ANNETTE. I have not asked any questions, miss.

LILIA. That is enough. . . . let me be quiet, go to your work. (*Annette starts to go out, and Lilia calls her back.*) Annette!

ANNETTE, (*returning.*) Miss!

LILIA. Go look for my hat.

ANNETTE. Yes, miss. (*She retires.*)

SCENE V.—*Lilia, alone.*

LILIA. How insipid and disagreeable is the society of these people! . . . . How common they are! . . . and this is the only company that I can have in this dull place. It is impossible to contract here any friendship, the young girls are so common, so badly reared! . . . I must see them, however, for mamma requires it. . . . . What a singular taste! Ah! how different is my situation from that of Zulma de Cérigny! She passes her life in the midst of pleasures, and the short visit

which she makes to the country is varied by a thous-
and diversions and the most amiable company. Her
mother knows how to maintain her rank, to say the
least of it.

Scene VI.—*Lilia—Annette.*

Annette, (*presenting the hat.*) Miss Lilia, here is
your hat.

Lilia. Very good.

Annette. It would give pleasure to your mother,
without doubt, if you go to meet her. I can accompany you.

Lilia. You fatigue me with your advice. Retire,
I wish to be alone.

Annette. Very good, miss. (*Retiring.*) What a
humor !

Scene VII.—*Lilia.*

Lilia. This girl is insupportable, she takes a tone
of authority which displeases me exceedingly. . . . The
familiarity of these people towards me, is one of the
effects of the manner in which I have been reared. I
have always been kept in a kind of dependence which
did not correspond with the rank I hold in society.

But now I am no child, and I will not suffer them
to be wanting in respect to me.

SCENE VIII.—*Lilia—Delphina—Virginia.*

DELPHINA. Good day, Miss Lilia, your mamma desired us to come to see you sometimes, and it is with much pleasure we accept her kind invitation.

LILIA, (*coldly.*) I am obliged to you, young ladies. Let us go into the house.

VIRGINIA. We are very well here, miss; you were taking the air, and we should be grieved to disturb you. Besides, the weather is so fine, it is more agreeable outside than shut up in a room.

DELPHINA. Do you like the country, miss?

LILIA. Not much, it is very dull.

DELPHINA. As for me, I love the country dearly; but that is not astonishing, as I was born here.

LILIA. You have, without doubt, never lived in the city?

DELPHINA. I beg your pardon, miss; I passed three years at school in Lyons. I spent a pleasant time there, because I had very good teachers and amiable companions; nevertheless, I was very happy when I returned home, never to leave it again.

VIRGINIA. It is so sweet to live in the midst of one's family! It is necessary to be deprived of this happiness, in order to appreciate it.

LILIA, (*aside, shrugging her shoulders.*) What an interesting conversation! (*Aloud.*) Of course, you amused yourself by going to the theatre in Lyons?

VIRGINIA. Oh! certainly not, miss, it is prohibited whilst we are at school, and, besides, our mamma maintains that young ladies ought not to go there.

LILIA. When the pieces are select, I do not see what harm there can be in it. Besides, every body, that is to say, all in high society, go to the theatre, and when we are in company, we must have something to talk about.

DELPHINA. Happily, we do not belong to high society, and we can well be ignorant of some things without being ridiculous.

LILIA. Without doubt; but I cannot say as much. (*Perceiving Margaret, who passes at the back of the stage.*) Who is that woman? I find her constantly on my path.

VIRGINIA. We know but little of her. We only know that she passes her life in deep sadness, caused, they say, by the loss of her husband and of her only child. She seldom goes out, and I believe that if her work did not force her, she would never go out.

LILIA. You astonish me, I find her everywhere. Is she poor?

DELPHINA. She is not rich; however, she has some ready money, and lives honestly by working.

LILIA. At what is she employed?

VIRGINIA. She works in the fields, and she occupies herself between times like all the women of the country.

LILIA. Was her child large when she lost her?

VIRGINIA. I believe not. I never saw her.

LILIA, (*sighing.*) Poor woman!

SCENE IX.—*The same—Lisetta.*

LISETTA, (*offering a bouquet to Lilia.*) Miss, will you accept this little bouquet of violets?

LILIA. Thank you, there is a quantity of them in the garden.

LISETTA. I suppose so, miss, but these were gathered in the woods; they smell so sweet.

LILIA. I understand; give them to me. (*She draws out her purse and presents a franc to her.*) Take this for your trouble.

LISETTA. What do you say, miss? I do not wish to sell them. Heaven preserve me from accepting money for so small a thing.

LILIA. If you do not take my money, I refuse your violets. You have not time to lose in gathering flowers.

LISETTA, (*running out.*) I will never take money for a few violets!

LILIA. This little girl vexes me! .... I do not like to receive presents.

DELPHINA. You would have given her much pain, miss, by refusing these flowers, which she culled with so much pleasure for you.

2

SCENE X.—*Lilia—Delphina—Virgina—Marietta.*

MARIETTA, (*entering.*) Ah! Miss Lilia! I have a little lamb which is as white as snow. You will see how pretty it is. When it is a little stronger, I will bring it to you.

LILIA. You may save yourself the trouble. What shall I do with it?

MARIETTA. You will raise it, miss, it will become accustomed to eat from your hand, and it will follow you everywhere.

LILIA. What a precious advantage! Preserve me from such a vexation! I do not like animals.

MARIETTA. But a little lamb is so pretty, so affectionate!

LILIA. Ah, well! keep it for yourself.

MARIETTA. Only accept it, miss, and I will come to look at it every day. It will not give you any trouble.

LILIA. I do not want it, I tell you! If it were to become mine, I would give it very quickly to any one who would take it from me.

MARIETTA. I am very sorry. I took so much pleasure in offering it to you. (*She goes out, looking very sad.*)

SCENE XI.—*Lilia—Delphina—Virginia.*

VIRGINIA. The poor little girl is quite disappointed. A lamb is much for her; and she believed it would be agreeable to you for her to offer it.

LILIA. All the people in this place believe I have tastes like theirs. They fatigue me with their homage and their presents.

DELPHINA. You must excuse them, miss, and see nothing in their eagerness but a desire to please you.

VIRGINIA. Your ancestors have done so much good in the country around, that every one would wish to testify the gratitude due to you.

LILIA. This they would be able to do more agreeably to me, by allowing me to be quiet. I am never alone.

DELPHINA. It is very true, miss, that it is very indiscreet in them to annoy you in this manner; and, for our part, we have abused your patience by detaining you so long. Will you excuse us?

LILIA, (*coloring.*) I pray you, young ladies, do not apply to yourselves the remarks I have made. Your visit has given me much pleasure.

VIRGINIA. The pleasure and the honor are ours, miss; but we ought not to abuse your indulgence. (*They go out.*)

LILIA. You really grieve me by leaving so soon, young ladies.

SCENE XII.—*Lilia, alone.*

LILIA. I fear I have offended them. They are really very good ; but, nevertheless, they are tiresome. One does not know how to converse with them, because they have not any of the customs of the world, and can only speak of the beauties of the country, beauties which do not charm me at all. However, they have interested me in talking of this extraordinary woman, whose maternal love is so deep and so durable. This solitude and this melancholy are really romantic ; and, if the miserable woman had been born in a high condition, she might certainly have been something remarkable ; but a defective education paralyzes the best disposi- tions. . . What a martyrdom always to be surrounded by such people ! and that during a whole summer ! It is enough to craze one ! . . . And, yet, I used to enjoy myself in the country, for it was with transports of joy that I started to pass the summer in the old and lone- some castle of Mont-Roc. Ah ! what a difference be- tween that old manor and its uncultivated surround- ings, and this beautiful modern castle, situated at the entrance of a pretty village, in a smiling and fertile plain ! . . . . Ah ! why have I changed so ? Anything amused me then, now I become tired everywhere. . . . Whence comes this sad change ? . . . .

SCENE XIII.—*Lilia—Margaret, with a covered basket on her arm.*

MARGARET, (*advancing timidly.*) Miss, here are two turtle-doves which I have raised, to offer to you. Will you be good enough to accept them?

LILIA. Very willingly, my good woman. Of all birds, I love only these. (*She uncovers the basket.*) Poor little things! how pretty they are! I thank you, you have given me much pleasure. (*She opens her purse and presents to her two five franc pieces.*) In your turn, accept this little sum.

MARGARET. Oh! miss, I cannot sell them. I am so happy to offer them to you, it would take away the pleasure, if you paid me for them.

LILIA. You will displease me also, if you will not accept anything.

MARGARET. Ah! miss, I will be amply paid, if you will . . . . . but no, I am foolish.

LILIA. Why do you stop? Fear nothing, speak.

MARGARET. No, no, miss, it would not be right.

LILIA. Speak without fear, I pray you, you interest me. I will refuse you nothing.

MARGARET. Indeed, miss, I will be the happiest person in the world, if you will permit me to embrace you.

LILIA. What an idea! You are not thinking of what you ask, my good woman. I am disposed to do

2*

for you whatever you wish; but I do not embrace any one but mamma.

MARGARET. Ah! miss, I feel I have committed an indiscretion. Will you pardon me, not hate me, and say nothing about it to Madame de St. Elme? (*Retiring, she says:*) Ah! I entreat you not to send back to me my turtle-doves?

SCENE XIV.—*Lilia, alone.*

LILIA. She is pained by my refusal! . . . . Poor woman! her grief wounds my heart. . . . Alas! I was born in this village; her daughter was, perhaps, of my age, and, by embracing me, she would imagine she was embracing her child. Why have I refused her this trifling favor? Her eyes were so soft, her look so suppliant! . . . . She follows me everywhere, she loves me, I am sure; by embracing her, I would have made her happy. . . . . It must be acknowledged, however, that the request was very indiscreet; a woman like her, to ask a kiss of a young lady of my rank! . . . . When Maria Theresa, that great empress of Germany, went on foot to visit a poor old woman who desired to see her, did she believe that she had derogated from the dignity of her rank? Oh! no indeed, she performed an act of charity, and that was all. And St. Elizabeth of Hungary, who tended the poor and dressed their wounds with her own hands, did she cease to do this because she was a great queen? No, she joined to this title that of a great saint and insured for herself an immortal crown. . . . Alas! I used also to be sweet and affable, like my dear mamma. I was loved then, I loved, and I was really most happy; but I am not so now. O Zulma! why did I ever share your luxury and your pleasures? What trouble you have cast upon my existence. . . . . . But these sad reflections are foolish! If I have pained this poor woman, it is easy for me to repair the harm done; some kind words will make her happy. . . . . She interests me. . . . Mrs. Roger, our housekeeper, has never left the country, she ought to know her. I will learn from her the condition of this poor creature, and if she is in want I will assist her. . . .

SCENE XV.—*Madame de St. Elme—Lilia—Miss Josephine.*

MADAME DE ST. ELME. You are alone, my Lilia. I was sorry you were not with us, you would have had a charming walk; the country is so beautiful at this season.

LILIA. I would have been happy to accompany you, mamma, because your society is very dear to me; but I do not regret the walk, for the country has no charms for me. Besides, I have not been alone during your absence. I have been really beset with visits and presents. Misses Virginia and Delphina were the first who came.

MADAME DE ST. ELME. I am very glad, for they are charming young girls.

LILIA, (*apart.*) What taste! (*Aloud.*) Then came a crowd of villagers. One gave me these violets; another, these turtle-doves; another offered me a lamb; and, in fact, I have not had an´ instant to myself.

MADAME DE ST. ELME. You ought to be very grateful for these testimonies of love and respect. . . . . But, my dear Josephine, you appear fatigued.

JOSEPHINE. You are right: I go out so little.

MADAME DE ST. ELME. Come and take some rest, my dear friend; let us return to the castle. Come, Lilia.

LILIA. With pleasure, mamma, I am never happier than when I am with you.

END OF THE FIRST ACT.

ACT II.

SCENE I.—*Lilia, alone.*

LILIA. What a dreadful night I have passed! ...
O fatal secret! ... Why did I wish to discover it? ..
Ah, me! This kind mother, who surrounded my
infancy with so many tokens of love, this mother
whom I love with all my soul, is a stranger to me,
and I owe my being to miserable creatures who have
sold me! Oh! misfortune, dreadful misfortune! ....
Death would be a thousand times preferable to my
sad existence. ... Yesterday morning, I awoke filled
with the sweetest illusions, with the most flattering
hopes. The name I bore was my glory, the prestige
of grandeur surrounded me, and now all has dis-
appeared, never to return. Birth, fortune, pleasures,
friendship .... nothing remains to me. I am a poor
creature, without a name, a thousand times lower in
my social position than those I have treated with so
much pride. .... However, this secret has been revealed only to me. .... I am mistress of it; but
what shall I do? ... Shall I remain in this castle,
usurping the homage which people believe they are
paying to the young lady of the house? Shall I give
orders as a mistress, whilst I am only a poor stranger?

Shall I be able, without shedding a torrent of tears, to give the name of mother to her who has always treated me with so much indulgence and love? . . . Ah! if I had always responded to her tenderness, my regret would be less bitter; but the love of pleasure, the spirit of domination, a thousand whims have often made me wanting in the respect a well reared girl ought to have for her mother. . . . . How many times have I not seen her shed tears whilst addressing to me her sweet exhortations or her tender reproaches! . . . . And I did not cast myself at her feet, I did not ask her a thousand pardons, and promise her to be better! In place of wiping away her tears, I have grieved her, by imitating the ostentatious friend of whose pleasures I have, for a short period, partaken. My tastes have always been opposed to hers. Ah! I well merit the sorrow which overwhelms me. (*After a moment's silence.*) This country place, which yesterday appeared so sad, would be cheerful to my eyes, if I could persuade myself that all I have heard was a dream! . . . . But, no, it is a dreadful reality. . . . . I am not the daughter of the excellent Madame de St. Elme; I owe my existence to Margaret, ... to Margaret, who loves me, who regrets me, and whose maternal embrace I have repelled. . . . . Unhappy mother! Still more unhappy daughter! . . . O my God! my God, take pity on me! . . . .

Scene II.—*Lilia—Mrs. Roger.*

Mrs. Roger. Poor Miss Lilia! How pale and dejected you look! how much I reproach myself for my culpable indiscretion! Why did I let slip that unlucky exclamation, when I heard you speak of your mother! and why, yielding to your entreaties, did I reveal to you a secret which I had sworn always to keep? The most severe prohibition has been given on the subject and the most rigorous punishment promised to whomever should reveal it. (*Striking her forehead.*) Oh! is it possible! after having kept it faithfully for fourteen years, I have let it slip at a moment when all was forgotten, and when Madame de St. Elme believed it would never be known!

Lilia. If I was born in this village, and lived in it for two years, this secret ceases to be one, it must be known by all the inhabitants.

Mrs. Roger. It is not known to any person. Your parents were strangers, and they lived in a little cabin at the entrance of the forest in which your father worked. I am sure the greater part of the villagers were ignorant of your existence. Since then the servants of the castle have all been changed, and every body believes you to be Miss de St. Elme. Besides, Madame de St. Elme left the country almost as soon as she had adopted you, and your mother has not seen you since she deposited you in the arms of the lady of the castle.

LILIA, (*wiping her eyes.*)   Ah! if death had stricken me at that moment, how happy I should have been!

MRS. ROGER.   Calm yourself, my dear miss.   After all, your lot is not changed; you will always be the adopted and beloved daughter of Madame de St. Elme, and, in the eyes of the world, you will always be the noble lady of the castle.

LILIA.   But am I such in my own eyes?   Can I receive, without a blush, the honors which are not due me?   Can I, without my heart breaking, see my mother follow me, look at me, without presuming to speak to me?

MRS. ROGER.   Your mother knows the conditions she made; she accepted them freely; and, notwithstanding the emotion which she experiences, her motherly love is flattered by beholding you rich, pretty, and well reared.

LILIA.   Her pale face and sad look do not appear as if these were her thoughts.

MRS. ROGER.   After having been so long without seeing you, her feelings at seeing you again, are but natural.   But believe me, she does not suffer as you think.   I was near Madame de St. Elme, when she placed you in her arms.   She pressed a kiss upon your forehead, and her features expressed more joy than grief.

LILIA.   I believe it, for she saved my father; but since his death, she is alone, abandoned. . .   No, no, it is impossible for me to allow her to remain longer in this . . . .

Mrs. Roger. Be discreet, I beg of you, my dear young lady, and do not let any one draw from you the fatal secret you have heard from me. You will cause much unhappiness. You would take away from Madame de St. Elme all the pleasure with which she looks upon you as her daughter, because she would know she is no longer the exclusive object of your affections; you would lose the consideration and respect of the servants of the castle and the inhabitants of the village, who honor you as Miss de St. Elme, whilst you are really only the daughter of a poor stranger. Margaret herself would gain nothing by this revelation; for, should Madame de St. Elme return you to her, what could she offer you in exchange for the kindness which you have received here? And, then, she is respected now as a good and quiet woman; but what would be said of her if it were known that she had sold her child? Madame de St. Elme would be very much displeased with her; had she not followed you so closely, you would never have known anything about the matter. In fine, I do not speak to you of my poor husband and myself. For twenty years we have possessed the confidence of our masters; we have served them faithfully, and now we would be driven away, undoubtedly, as wretches! Ah! miss, do not cause all this trouble. Have pity on us, I beg of you...... You answer nothing?

Lilia. What do you wish me to answer? O what unhappiness!

3

Mrs. Roger. This unhappiness is not without a remedy, my dear young lady. You will cheer the days of Madame de St. Elme, by your care, attention, and your love. You will make your immense riches serve for the good of your fellow-creatures, and when your age and position render you mistress of your actions, you will heap wealth and favors upon your mother, who will then receive the recompense of the sacrifice which she made in living far from you. In this manner, nothing will be changed, and every body will be contented.

Lilia. The others would be contented, perhaps. I, never!

Mrs. Roger. The happiness of others would make you happy. (*With a supplicating look.*) You will say nothing about it, will you? (*Lilia remains silent.*) My good young lady, I beseech you on my knees. (*She falls on her knees.*)

Lilia. Ah! well, yes, I promise you, I will be silent.

Mrs. Roger. Of what a weight you have relieved me! O miss, I leave you, for some one might perceive our long conversation, but I go tranquil, I have your word, and I can count . . . .

Lilia, (*interrupting her.*) Yes, yes.

Scene III.—*Lilia, alone.*

LILIA. What promise have I made? . . . . . Will
it be possible for me to keep it? Will I be mistress
of the emotions of my heart, and can I resume the
tranquil routine of my life, as if I were ignorant of
all? . . . . This is, however, the only reasonable part
to take; trouble, disorder, unhappiness of all kinds,
would be the inevitable fruit of a revelation. . . . . .
Poor mamma! would that I could in reality tell you
that I love you, that I respect you, that you are my
all; but I know that I do not belong to you, and the
deep love which I feel for you is founded on gratitude,
but it is no longer a filial love. The kiss which you
press every night on my forehead, is no longer a
maternal kiss. This maternal kiss I have refused
with contempt, and the unhappy person who gave me
birth was repulsed by my arms. . . . . Why did she
cast me from hers? Why did she not expose herself
to all the horrors of misery, in order to keep her child
near her? . . . Alas! poor woman! it was necessary to
resign her child or to sacrifice her husband. She saved
the one and secured for the other a happy existence and
careful education, when she intrusted her to the good
Madame de St. Elme, the tutelary angel of the country.
She deprived herself only of the pleasure, so sweet for
a mother, of seeing her daughter grow up under her
eyes and of enjoying her caresses. She has felt all

the horrors of this privation; her paleness, her sadness, her assiduity in following me, have said enough. .... How much she was grieved yesterday on leaving me! Her languishing eyes turned from time to time to see me again; she loves me still, in spite of my harshness. And shall I leave her in this sad state? .... Shall I not go and offer her, or ask of her, the kiss which she desired? Oh! yes, I will fly to her, she shall feel the heart of her daughter beat on hers; she shall see that religion and nature have not lost their right over my heart. .... I will abandon you then, my dear and good adopted mother? You, who have shed so many charms upon my existence? ... The reward of your care will be abandonment, at the moment when you believe yourself about to enjoy the gratitude of your daughter, become of an age to appreciate your love? .... This ungrateful daughter will leave you without having repaired the trouble which she has caused you since her fatal change? No, no, this sacrifice is beyond my strength. O my two mothers! .... What shall I do? .... My heart is broken, I can do nothing. O my God, aid me, enlighten me. Holy Virgin, august Mother of the Son of God, consolatrix of the afflicted, do not abandon me, support me!

SCENE IV.—*Madame de St. Elme—Lilia.*

MADAME DE ST. ELME. You are down in good time, this morning, Lilia. . . . But, what do I see? Why this paleness, these tears? What ails you, my beloved daughter?

LILIA. O my tender mother! My dear benefactress! (*Falling on her knees.*)

MADAME DE ST. ELME, (*raising her.*) What are you saying, my daughter? What do these words signify?

LILIA. Pardon my trouble and the disorder in which I appear before you, O you, whom I love more than my life! I wished to hide from you the grief which oppresses me, not to let you know the terrible discovery which I have made. I have not been able to do so. I am not then your daughter! O how unhappy I am?

MADAME DE ST. ELME. Unfortunate child! Your mother has then revealed this fatal secret to you.

LILIA. My unhappy mother has said nothing to me; but her assiduity in keeping near me everywhere, her sweet, sad look have interested me; I wanted to know who this singular woman was: I have questioned, pressed, ... and I know.

MADAME DE ST. ELME. Mrs. Roger alone could have told you. But what induced you to question her so closely? What doubts could have arisen in your mind?

3*

LILIA. I had not any doubt, my good mother, but this woman excited my curiosity; and not having any one to ask but Mrs. Roger, I questioned her, expressing my surprise at the woman's persistence in following me. An exclamation escaped her, I wished to know more, and by dint of entreaty, I have learned all. O fatal moment!

MADAME DE ST. ELME, (*aside.*) O Divine Providence! (*Aloud.*) I hoped to carry this secret to the grave and enjoy in my old age your filial tenderness. God has ordained otherwise, I must submit. . . . But what will you do, Lilia? You cannot have two mothers; with which do you wish to stay?

LILIA. Ah! could I leave you without dying? Your presence and your love are as necessary to me as the air I breathe. It would be impossible for me to live far from you.

MADAME DE ST. ELME. Ah! well, my daughter, my Lilia, you shall be always near me. No one shall know the secret which has caused your tears; we will leave to-morrow. I will sell this place and never return to it again.

LILIA. Never! . . . . . And shall this unhappy mother search in vain for the only child God has given her? Shall she never hear a word of love from her mouth? Condemned by poverty to the severest privations, not knowing the joys of the world, shall she always be deprived of the happiness which the poorest of mothers experience near their children?

MADAME DE ST. ELME. Are your words reproaches, Lilia? Do you begrudge the caresses which
you have lavished on me, and which have made my
heart beat with joy? You can go to her, my benefits
shall follow you there, and you can indemnify her for
the long privation which she has endured.

LILIA. And I would be far from you, whose love
has anticipated all my desires, who have imparted so
much sweetness to my life. To leave you who possess
all my heart, is impossible. I will follow you everywhere! Ah! poor mother! if you had only once felt
the heart of your daughter beating against your own;
if your maternal love had only once received a trifling
return; if you had received the kiss which you desired
with so much ardor! .... But no.

MADAME DE ST. ELME, (interrupting her.) What
kiss? What do you mean?

LILIA. Alas! my good mother, shall I be able to
tell you without blushing? .... My poor mother
brought me the turtle-doves which I showed you
yesterday. I wished to pay her for them; she refused
to take the money. I insisted. Then she tremblingly
asked of me the permission to embrace me, but with
an air so humble, so tender, that my heart is racked
when I think that I had the cruelty to refuse her.

MADAME DE ST. ELME, (aside.) Poor mother!
poor daughter! (aloud.) I have a means of arranging
the affair and of reconciling duty and affection. I consent to live here, you can remain with me and can see

your mother every day. But, you must feel that, as
the daughter of Margaret, you cannot have in my
house the rank you have occupied until now. The
servants will not easily submit to a young girl of their
own condition; your old companions knowing your
birth, will probably look at you with another eye;
they will no longer consider you their equal; you can
only be a young country girl, the first among the
servants of the castle.

LILIA. And what matters the rank I occupy, since
I cannot believe myself to be your daughter? I will
be near you—I will be able to lavish on you my care,
my love, to show you that I was not wholly un-
deserving of your bounty. I know your heart, you
will permit me to call you, in secret, my mother, my
good and tender mother, you will sometimes press me
to your heart and call me your daughter, your dear
Lilia; could I then be unhappy? Oh, no!

MADAME DE ST. ELME. Your heart and your
imagination mislead you, poor child. You see the fair
side of your position; but have you reflected on what
you will have to suffer from the disdain of your old
companions, from the change which will necessarily
take place in the manners of the people of the castle
and of the inhabitants of the village, who, no longer
seeing in you Miss de St. Elme, will not have the
same regard for you, and will revenge themselves,
perhaps, for your past pride? In fine, what will you
think, on seeing the other young ladies, dressed with

taste, admired in company, and enjoying all the pleasures which you will not have?

LILIA. The unhappiness which smites me has re-
moved the veil which concealed the danger and illusions of the world from me, and if anything can console
me for the misfortune of not being your daughter, it
will be the insurmountable barrier which has raised
itself between that world and me. O my good mother!
(permit me to use this sweet name,) if I had never
tasted its foolish joys, I would never have caused your
tears to flow. Oh! pardon me, I beg you! The dis-
comforts of my new position will seem sweet to me,
whilst thinking that they expiate my past pride; and
the holy family joys which I did not appreciate, are
henceforth the only thing I wish for. The rest is
nothing in my eyes.

MADAME DE ST. ELME. Calm yourself, Lilia; re-
flect before taking an irrevocable resolution on which
your future depends. You are now in a state of ex-
citement which will not permit you to see things as
they are. Retire; pray God to enlighten you. I
want to be alone. Send Annette to me.

LILIA, (*going out.*) Always love your poor Lilia.

MADAME DE ST. ELME, (*alone.*) Poor child! this
trial costs me as much as yourself. Ah! may your
mother prove herself . . . . .

SCENE V.—*Madame de St. Elme—Annette.*

ANNETTE, (*entering.*) What do you wish, madam?

MADAME DE ST. ELME. Go tell Margaret, the widow woman who lives in the thatched cottage, at the edge of the woods, that I wish to speak to her.

ANNETTE. This is, without doubt, the woman who is almost wild, and never speaks to any person, and who is so very strange in every way.

MADAME DE ST. ELME. Yes, it is she. Go. (*Annette goes out.*)

SCENE VI.—*Madame de St. Elme, alone.*

MADAME DE ST. ELME. How will she take the confidence I am going to repose in her? Ah! may she show herself the worthy mother of my dear Lilia! O my God! it is Thou who hast prepared this trial,— assist me! May I make two beings happy and still be agreeable to Thee! Pardon me this long enjoyment which I have tasted alone, and which was beginning to bring such bitter results. Put in our hearts Thy peace, the only true happiness to be desired on earth. (*She walks about in silence.*)

SCENE VII.—*Madame de St. Elme—Annette.*

ANNETTE, (*entering.*) Margaret will be here in a moment.

MADAME DE ST. ELME. Very well, go to my room. When I want you, I will call you.

ANNETTE. Very well, madam. (*She goes out.*)

MADAME DE ST. ELME. The decisive moment has come. I tremble at what I am going to discover. O my God, give me the courage which I need; I can do nothing without Thee!

SCENE VIII.—*Madame de St. Elme—Margaret.*

MARGARET. Miss Annette told me you wished to speak to me, madam.

MADAME DE ST. ELME. Yes, Margaret. You remember the arrangement which we made together fourteen years ago?

MARGARET, (*sighing.*) Yes, madam.

MADAME DE ST. ELME. You know that then you resigned to me all your rights over your daughter, and that you promised me to keep her birth an inviolable secret?

MARGARET. I have not forgotten it, madam; and notwithstanding the tumultuous feelings which have risen in my heart on seeing her, I have not broken my promise?

MADAME DE ST. ELME. Do you repent of your promise?

MARGARET. Ah! madam, in depriving myself of the love and caresses of my daughter, I have debarred myself the only joy I might have hoped to find on earth; but by this sacrifice, I saved her father from an unhappiness which he dreaded more than death. It is true, I have lost him since, and his death has left me in a state of complete isolation; but I nursed him in his last sickness, and religion procured for him the succour and consolation of which he would probably have been deprived in a strange country. I believe, therefore, that I did my duty in giving up my dear child. Consequently, madam, I do not repent of what I have done.

MADAME DE ST. ELME. I have repented, Margaret, whilst feeling the sweet emotions which ought to have been yours. I have regretted having deprived you of the only happiness you might have on earth; and the desire to see you, to know your position, and your sentiments, made me decide to come and pass the summer in this part of the country, which I had abandoned.

MARGARET. You are very good, madam. Without doubt, the thought of my daughter is the only one which occupies me in my solitude; but this dear child is better with you than with me, madam, for she is receiving an education which I could not give her. She has before her eyes your virtuous example; and, in a word, she is happy, good, and pious. What a consolation for me. . . . .

MADAME DE ST. ELME. Yes, she is happy. Her desires are all anticipated, and my love, which is truly a mother's love, has given her all that a great name and immense riches can command; but her piety and virtue might have been more secure, perhaps, in the cabin than in the castle. The conveniences of rank entail pleasures in which the most solid virtues are sometimes wrecked.

MARGARET. Ah! madam, I beg you to watch over her. She is a sacred deposit which I have placed in your hands. Preserve in her the precious treasure of innocence, compared with which other treasures are nothing. Do not cause her unhappy mother to feel a mortal regret for the sacrifice imposed upon her by her sad position. I can, with the grace of God, bear the indifference of my daughter; but it would kill me to see her exposed to losing the virtues she now possesses. . . . Ah! madam, I beg of you, let her be poor, miserable, if it is necessary, but let her never forget her duty.

MADAME DE ST. ELME. Excellent woman! you well merit what I intend to do for you. (*She calls.*) Annette.

SCENE IX.—*The same—Annette.*

ANNETTE, (*entering.*) What do you wish, madam?

MADAME DE ST. ELME. Tell Miss Lilia to come down.

4

ANNETTE. Yes, madam. (*She goes out.*)

MARGARET. Madam, what are you going to do?
(*Aside.*) I tremble.

MADAME DE ST. ELME. You will soon know.

SCENE X.—*Madame de St. Elme—Margaret—Lilia.*

LILIA, (*entering quickly and throwing herself into her
mother's arms.*) My mother, my good mother! I
have then refused your maternal kiss!.... Pardon
me, I did not know you.

MARGARET, (*much moved.*) My dear daughter!...
Miss, what are you doing?

LILIA, (*looking at Madame de St. Elme.*) You permit it, do you not, O you who have been the most
tender of mothers, you, by whom I have been taught
what duty and virtue are?

MADAME DE ST. ELME. Yes, my dear daughter, I
do permit it. You are worthy of each other, you shall
never be separated again.

MARGARET. Ah! poor child!.... Can she become accustomed ....

MADAME DE ST. ELME. Be tranquil, Margaret.
Lilia shall be always with me, without being separated
from you. You shall never again leave us. It is
time for you to be restored to the happiness of which
I have deprived you. Mrs. Roger has yielded to a
culpable indiscretion; I cannot keep her at the castle.

You can take her place, and during our sojourn here, which will be every year during the summer, you will see your daughter every hour of the day.

LILIA. Ah! my dear mamma, how happy I would be, were it not for the unhappiness of Mrs. Roger! She yielded to my earnest entreaties. What will become of her?

MARGARET. The place which you propose to give me, madam, would fulfil all my desires; but could I be happy in taking the place of two old persons who have served you faithfully during so many years, particularly when my daughter caused their removal?

MADAME DE ST. ELME. You are a perfect woman, Margaret. Mrs. Roger shall keep her office, and you shall not leave us. You will be not my house-keeper, but my friend. You shall have at the castle a room, where you can follow the modest habits of your former life. You will be as free as you please. Lilia will be my daughter and yours at the same time. She will keep her rank, and her loving heart will be the joy of both mothers. (*Margaret and Lilia fall on their knees, Madame de St. Elme raises them up.*)

MARGARET. Ah! madam, what kindness!

LILIA. O dear mother, if you could see the joy which overflows my soul, how much consolation your heart would feel! You have done every thing for your adopted daughter, and by restoring me to my mother you have completed your bounty. My heart cannot express my gratitude. May God pour down upon you

His sweetest benedictions! By Him only can our debt of gratitude towards you be paid.

MARGARET. I will pray for this as long as I live. O God Almighty, aid me! I cannot stand the excess of my joy.

LILIA. Bear up, my dear mother, keep your health and strength to love your daughter and her noble benefactress.

SCENE XI.—*The same—Miss Josephine.*

MISS JOSEPHINE, (*as she enters.*) What do I see?

MADAME DE ST. ELME. Come in, my friend, come share my happiness. I wished to try my adopted daughter, but I did not have the courage. Providence has come to my assistance. It has arranged a trial which has given me a full knowledge of her. Thank God, she is worthy of the lot I had designed for her. The world had fascinated her mind, but it had not corrupted her heart. She is mine, and soon she will belong to me by indissoluble ties. O, my friend, now I am happy!

JOSEPHINE. I congratulate you with all my heart, dear friend, but I do not understand what I hear and see. Yesterday, you were so unhappy!

LILIA. Ah! mamma, how can I repair . . . .

MADAME DE ST. ELME, (*interrupting her.*) Do not speak of it any more, all is forgotten. But we are all three crying. Lilia lead your mother to your room, and you, dear friend, come into mine. I will tell you what God has done to dry my tears and to calm my trouble, and you will assist me in returning thanks.

MARGARET. May God be blessed for having re-united mother and daughter under the protection of the most noble heart that ever beat!